DINOSAUR HABITAT

Helen V. Griffith
Dinosaur
Habitat

ILLUSTRATIONS BY SONJA LAMUT

GREENWILLOW BOOKS  NEW YORK

Text copyright © 1998 by Helen V. Griffith
Illustrations copyright © 1998 by Sonja Lamut
All rights reserved. No part of this book
may be reproduced or utilized in any form
or by any means, electronic or mechanical,
including photocopying, recording, or by
any information storage and retrieval
system, without permission in writing
from the Publisher, Greenwillow Books,
a division of William Morrow & Company, Inc.,
1350 Avenue of the Americas, New York, NY 10019.
Printed in the United States of America
First Edition
1 2 3 4 5 6 7 8 9 10

Library of Congress Cataloging-in-Publication Data
Griffith, Helen V.
Dinosaur habitat / by Helen V. Griffith ;
pictures by Sonja Lamut.
p.   cm.
Summary: After twelve-year-old Nathan's pesky
younger brother Ryan claims to have found a
dinosaur fossil, they are suddenly transported into
a misty world where Ryan's toy dinosaurs are alive.
ISBN 0-688-15324-0
[1. Dinosaurs—Fiction.
2. Time travel—Fiction.
3. Brothers—Fiction.]
I. Lamut, Sonja, ill.   II. Title.
PZ7.G8823Di   1998
[Fic]—dc21   97-10000   CIP   AC

For the Leamer boys

CONTENTS

DINOSAUR HABITAT

1: SILENCE

The wet green world was silent and still. Nothing moved but the water drops that slid down moss-covered trunks and dripped from the tips of branches. Ferns were everywhere, some tiny and delicate, others as tall as trees. There were creepers, too, and twining vines, and bushy clumps of grasses and reeds.

A lake, its surface as smooth as glass, lay in the midst of the swampy world. Beyond the lake rose a mountain, its rough black sides forming a perfect cinder cone. But no smoke poured from its vent. No rumbling sounds came from its depths. The volcano slept.

Across the lake a high cliff of reddish brown stone reached toward the sky. Near the top of the cliff was a ledge, and hunched on the ledge was a creature with wings like a bird. But instead of feathers, it had brilliant red skin. Instead of a beak, it had toothy, pointed jaws. It sat without stirring, as still as the rock on which it perched.

Half submerged in the shallows of the blue lake lay a barrel-shaped animal of an even brighter blue. The animal had four paddle-like flippers capable of propelling it swiftly through the water. But no ripples disturbed the surface of the glassy lake. No shadowy shape cut through the drifting underwater plants. The flippers floated motionless.

A creature with an odd bony frill across the back of its neck stood at the edge of the lake. It seemed about to walk into the water and dip its horned snout for a drink. But the creature never moved. It remained in place like a glossy black statue, its two long brow horns glistening with moisture.

A little distance from the lake an animal with yellow, pebbly skin and a flat snout appeared to be standing guard beside a depression in the swampy ground. But its head never turned. Its eyes stared blankly. It made no effort to see what might be lurking nearby. If it had, it would have discovered the small, sharp-faced creature that crouched in the undergrowth, as green as the vegetation that concealed it. And just as still.

Deeper in the wet woods another swamp dweller, this one a startling orange color, stood quietly. With its long, snaky neck it had the ability to reach the treetops. It could easily have feasted on the very highest leaves. But its mouth never opened. The leaves remained untouched.

Strangest of all, far from the other inhabitants of the swampy world, a glittering golden beast balanced on strong hind legs, its long, sharp talons piercing the marshy earth. A massive head and daggerlike teeth gave it a dangerous appearance. But no sound came from the powerful jaws. The animal was as motionless as everything else in the quiet swamp.

Drops of water plopped from branches onto the bodies of the strange, colorful creatures. But not a head turned. Not an eye blinked.

The humid air, the warm temperature, the lush vegetation seemed to create a perfect environment for the animals that inhabited it. Yet, except for the dripping water, nothing moved. For the moment, at least, everything was still.

2: NATHAN

Nathan stomped into the house late and mad. He was late because he had stopped off on the way home from school to shoot a few baskets. He was mad because he had to get home to keep an eye on his younger brother. Every day. That meant that he missed out on everything that happened after school. It was because Mom had a job now and didn't want Ryan coming home to an empty house.

"What about me?" Nathan had asked her when she made the rule. "Don't you worry about *me* coming home to an empty house?"

Mom had smiled, but Nathan wasn't kidding. "Well, when will Ryan be old enough to come home to an empty house?" he asked.

"When he's your age," Mom said.

"Ryan's only eight," Nathan protested. "He won't be my age for a hundred years."

"More like four," his mother said. "I'd better have a talk with your math teacher."

Nathan didn't laugh. He never felt like laughing these days, at least not when he was home. He didn't have a life of his own now that Mom was working. He had been turned into an unpaid baby-sitter.

The house was quiet. As Nathan walked to his bed to dump his book bag, he tripped over one of the books Ryan left lying everywhere. "Ryan!" he yelled angrily, but there was no answer. He yelled again. Ryan should have been home by now. Nathan wondered if he had been here and then been afraid to enter the house with no one there. Maybe he was wandering around the neighborhood telling everyone how his brother had deserted him.

As Nathan started to leave the bedroom, he stumbled over the book again. Angrily he kicked it out of the way. It skidded across the room and smacked against Ryan's terrarium, where it sat on the floor under the window. The jolt caused a rain shower in

the terrarium. Water dripped from the plants and ran down the glass sides.

The lid had been knocked off by the impact, and Nathan went over to replace it. He knew Ryan would notice and go running to Mom if he thought Nathan had touched his terrarium. He was very particular about it, checking the plants every day and adjusting the cover to control the amount of air and moisture. He had made a little tropical world full of thriving green plants.

There were animals in the terrarium, too, but unlike the plants, they weren't alive, and they weren't anything you would find in the tropics or anywhere else. They were little plastic dinosaurs.

Since Ryan wasn't around to yell, Nathan reached down into the terrarium. The air inside felt warm on his hand. He picked up one of the dinosaurs, a yellow one. All of the animals were brightly colored, much more gaudy than those in the dozens of dinosaur reference books Ryan was always leafing through.

Suddenly it occurred to Nathan that Ryan was very late. Something must be wrong. He dropped the dinosaur back into the terrarium and hurriedly replaced the lid. Why was he letting time go by? He should have done something as soon as he'd seen that Ryan wasn't home.

He ran to the phone. He should call Mom. But what could she do? Ryan's friends. He would start with them. They were the ones most likely to know where he was.

Nathan's hands were shaking as he searched through the phone book for a number to call. He had just dropped the book for the second time when there was a loud banging at the door. He ran to answer it, sure that it was bad news.

3: RYAN

It was Ryan. "Hi, Nathan," he said brightly. "I couldn't open the door because my hands are full of books because my book bag is full of neat things. Wait until you see."

For a minute Nathan felt weak with relief. His brother was okay. Then he was mad. Ryan shouldn't have scared him like that. "Where have you been?" he demanded.

"Did you forget about my science class field trip?" Ryan asked.

Nathan *had* forgotten. He could have stayed out for another half hour if he'd remembered. For some reason that made him even madder at Ryan.

Ryan had dropped his books and was opening his book bag. Nathan brushed past him and went back to their room. He flopped down on his bed, disgusted with himself and with Ryan, too.

Ryan grabbed his book bag and followed. "I have something to show you," he said. He rooted through his book bag, which seemed to be crammed with little green plants. "They're for my terrarium," he said, "but look at this, Nathan. Look what I found today." He pulled out a small whitish gray rock and displayed it proudly.

"This may surprise you," Nathan said, "but I've seen rocks before."

"This isn't just a rock," Ryan said importantly. "It's

a fossil." He forced it into Nathan's hand.

Nathan sat on the edge of the bed and looked it over. "Rock. Fossil. What's the difference?" he said.

"The difference is," Ryan said patiently, "that this rock was something else before it became a rock."

"That's nice," Nathan said.

Nathan tried to hand the rock back to Ryan, but Ryan said, "Look at it. Don't you see what it is?"

"Didn't you just tell me it was a fossil?" Nathan asked.

"But it's a special kind. Try to guess," Ryan said.

Nathan sighed. He couldn't be less interested, but he saw that he would have to guess just to shut Ryan up.

"A prehistoric hockey puck," he said. "An ancient baseball."

Ryan took the guesses seriously. "Wrong," he said. He took the little rock from Nathan and looked at it admiringly. "This rock," he said in a solemn voice, "is actually a fossilized egg."

"An egg," Nathan said skeptically. "What laid it, a dinochicken?" He snatched the rock from Ryan's hand and examined it. "This is no egg," he said.

"Well, not a whole egg," Ryan said.

"It's not even a yolk," Nathan said.

"I know it's not a yolk," Ryan said. "It's an eggshell. Part of an eggshell. It's a little piece from a big dinosaur egg."

Nathan ran his fingers over the fragment. As far as he could tell, it was a curved, rough-textured ordinary rock.

"What makes you so sure this is a dinosaur egg?" he asked.

"I can just tell," Ryan said. "My teacher said it isn't, but he doesn't know as much about dinosaurs as I do."

"Of course," Nathan said. "You're the great dinosaur expert of the world."

He was being sarcastic, but it was a waste of effort. Ryan just said, "I know." Then he crouched beside the terrarium, removed the lid, and took a deep breath. "Ah. Prehistoric air," he said. He reached inside the box and carefully pinched off some withered fern fronds. Then he gently picked up the black dinosaur standing by the pond.

"Okay, triceratops, I think you've had enough to

drink," he said. He put it down under a palm tree away from the water. "It's coelophysis's turn now." He moved the small green dinosaur from the bushes to the lakeside.

"Ryan," Nathan said, "I hate to be the one to tell you this, but those animals aren't alive. They don't get thirsty, and even if they did, they wouldn't be able to take a drink because they can't move."

"I know that," Ryan said. "I'm the one who bought them."

"You should get an ant farm," Nathan said. "At least ants can get around on their own."

Ryan looked shocked. "Anybody can have an ant farm," he said. "All you need is some dirt. What I've made here is a world. A real, living prehistoric world. The perfect habitat for my dinosaurs."

"Your dinosaurs are plastic," Nathan said. "Anyplace would be perfect habitat for them, except maybe a bonfire."

"They love it here," Ryan said confidently. "And if they weren't plastic, they would still love it." He sniffed the terrarium air again, then stood up. "Inside this box it's exactly the way things were when dinosaurs lived on the earth for real," he said. "I got dirt from a real marsh, and the plants in there are descended from plants that were here back then. The glass on the top keeps the temperature warm and steamy, and I even built a mountain, see? And not just an ordinary mountain, either. It's a volcano."

Ryan stood with his arms folded, admiring his work. Then he looked closer, frowning. "You've been messing with my terrarium," he said.

4: FOSSIL

Nathan raised his eyebrows in fake surprise. "Have I really?" he asked. "How can you tell. Did I leave footprints?"

"You moved my hadrosaur." Ryan reached inside the box and righted the yellow dinosaur that Nathan had dropped. "You're not supposed to touch my things," he said.

"Whose room is this?" Nathan asked.

"It's not just yours anymore," Ryan said. They'd had this argument a lot lately, and he knew all the answers. "It's half mine, and I can keep my things in here and you're not allowed to touch them."

"It's impossible to turn around in here without touching your stuff." Nathan was trying to be cool, but he was beginning to feel angry. Since Mom had taken Ryan's bedroom for her office, he didn't have any privacy at all.

"One little terrarium doesn't take up much room," Ryan said.

"That terrarium is gigantic," Nathan said, "and you can't walk across the room without stepping on plastic toys and lizard books."

"They're not toys," Ryan said, starting to get upset. "They're replicas of actual dinosaurs that lived on this earth years and years ago. And they aren't lizard books. They're all about dinosaurs, and they're very interesting. And the terrarium isn't gigantic, but it's still perfect dinosaur habitat."

"Perfect mold habitat," Nathan said. "Here, take your hard-boiled egg."

He tossed the rock to Ryan and threw himself back on his pillows. Ryan made a grab, but he missed. The rock flew past him and plopped into the center of the terrarium. It sank into the soft muck, knocking down several of Ryan's carefully planted ferns.

Right away Ryan started yelling. "Look what you did! You messed up my terrarium! I'm telling!"

Then his voice faded into silence. He stared at the part of the rock still visible above the mud. Nathan sat up and stared, too.

The rock was smoking. Thick grayish white clouds were pouring from its surface. No fire was visible, but it looked as if flames would burst forth at any moment.

As they watched, the smoke rolled across the bottom of the box and began to drift upward.

"What did you do?" Ryan whispered.

5: MIST

"I didn't do anything." Nathan noticed that he was whispering, too, and forced himself to speak louder. "Something's on fire in there."

"How could there be a fire?" Ryan was still whispering. "What would start a fire? Everything's wet."

The swirling smoke quickly swallowed up the dinosaurs and moved to the tops of the tallest plants. It billowed out of the terrarium and began to spread throughout the room. Suddenly smoke was all that Nathan could see.

"Let's get out of here," he yelled, but as soon as he got off the bed, he was lost. Which way was the door? The smoke was so thick he could barely make out his own arms.

"Ryan, where are you?" he shouted. "Get out of the smoke!" But as he was saying the words, it dawned on him that what he was breathing wasn't smoke at all. He wasn't choking or coughing. And there was no smoky smell in the air, only an outdoorsy odor of dampness and moss and leaves.

"It's just mist," Nathan thought wonderingly. "The room is full of mist." He called out, "We're okay, Ryan. It's not a fire." But Ryan didn't answer.

He must have found his way out. Good, now Nathan had only himself to worry about. He was relieved that he wasn't in danger of being suffocated, but not being able to see anything except mist was giving him a closed-in feeling that he didn't like.

He headed in what he hoped was the direction of the door. With each careful step he felt water seeping through his shoes, and he suspected uneasily that he had cracked the terrarium when he kicked the book into it. His mind immediately began working on an excuse to give his mother when Ryan told on him.

He stumbled over a soft lump on the floor and then another one. Probably some of Ryan's books, soaked to a pulp. More for Nathan to get in trouble over. The floor seemed uneven all of a sudden, and the rug felt spongy and very wet, much wetter than a leaky terrarium could make it.

Nathan was trying to keep calm, but he should

have come up to something by now, if not the door, at least a wall. And why was it so warm in here? His face was wet with sweat.

The damp, woodsy odor was stronger than ever, but now, mingled with it, came a strong, nose-tickling smell that caused a chill to run down Nathan's back. He had never come across that smell before, yet he knew what it was. It was the scent of a wild animal. And it was close.

Suddenly, unexpectedly, Nathan panicked. Arms stretched out in front of him, yelling at the top of his voice, he ran, slipping and stumbling, into the mysterious mist.

He ran until he collided with something tall and springy. It dipped with his weight, then sprang upright again, throwing him to the ground. The thud knocked the breath out of him. He had to stop yelling, and that helped him calm down a little.

Something else helped calm him, too. The mist was thinning. Nathan could see shapes now. The problem was, they weren't the shapes he wanted to see, like beds or desks or chairs. "This isn't my bedroom," Nathan thought as the lifting fog revealed a

forest of dripping vegetation. "This isn't our house. It's not even our yard."

The ground where Nathan lay was damp and mucky. The air was warm and steamy. He seemed to be in the middle of a vast swamp, and he was all alone.

He stood and tried to brush off some of the muck, but he just smeared it around. Then he wondered why he was worrying about a little dirt. He had a much bigger problem than muddy clothes. And he wasn't even sure what the problem was because he didn't know what had happened. Where was he? And where was Ryan?

He was starting to get scared again, but he couldn't afford to be scared. If he was scared, he couldn't think, and if he couldn't think, he wouldn't be able to figure out what was going on and what to do about it.

He stood still, breathing deeply to steady himself, as he watched the mist drift away. Now he could see massive tree trunks anchored in soggy dark earth and lots of ferns and palms and creeping vines. The world that was uncovered was a place where Nathan had never been before. But it was a familiar place. His heart began to thump uncomfortably as he realized just how familiar it all was.

"It's just like Ryan's terrarium," he thought, "only a whole lot bigger."

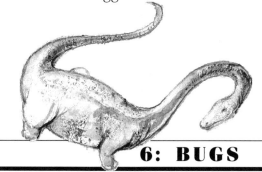

6: BUGS

Nathan started breathing hard again. He felt very scared. Then he became aware of scratching sounds in the undergrowth and rustling in the leaves overhead. He began to suspect that he wasn't as alone as he seemed.

A shrill screech burst from behind a clump of low palms. It was joined by another screech and then another and another. Screeching, rasping sounds came from all sides, and Nathan felt panic overwhelming him again.

"Ryan!" he screamed.

At his voice the screeching stopped. The foliage

rustled and shook with the slithering and sliding away of things that Nathan couldn't see.

Something in the undergrowth at his feet heaved itself up onto spindly legs and scuttled across the ground. Nathan lurched out of the way and fell against a rough tree trunk. He reached out to balance himself and almost grabbed a large, beady-eyed insect that was clinging to the bark.

It was one fright too many. Nathan yelled and threw himself to the ground. He rolled himself into a ball and covered his head with his arms. The insect flew away, its wings making a loud whir, but Nathan stayed where he was.

He crouched there for a long time, long enough for the dampness to soak through his clothes and for all the screechers, whatever they were, to think that he had gone and begin to screech again. He couldn't make himself get up. He couldn't face another giant creepy-crawly.

He began to worry about Ryan. He had yelled for him when he was scared, and now he wondered why. What could Ryan do? Anyway, he hadn't answered. Did that mean he wasn't here, wherever here was?

Could he be safe at home, wondering what had become of his big brother? Or was he hiding, alone and afraid, somewhere in this swamp?

"If I'm scared," Nathan thought, "how must Ryan feel?"

He had to get up, he knew that. He had promised to look out for Ryan, and he would, although he hadn't expected to be baby-sitting in a buggy bog.

He was still trying to force himself to stand up and look around when he noticed the vibrations. Where his body was in contact with the ground, he could feel a faint shake, a pause, then another shake. Each shake was a little stronger than the one before.

Nathan's heart began to thump uncomfortably as he realized what was causing those vibrations. Foot-steps, slow, careful footsteps were coming closer and closer, and they weren't bug footsteps, either. This was something a lot bigger than a bug.

7: TERRARIUM

Nathan's heart was pounding so hard it seemed about to choke him. He was afraid to move, yet he knew he couldn't just huddle there and let whatever was coming get him without a fight. But when, with a fierce shout, he jumped to his feet, it wasn't some killer monster he was facing. It was his little brother.

"Yike!" Ryan yelped. "Nathan, you scared me."

"Well, what are you sneaking around for?" Nathan hoped Ryan wouldn't notice how he was shaking.

"I didn't want to chase what you were looking at," Ryan said. "What *were* you looking at?"

"Bugs," Nathan said. It was sort of true. There was no way he would admit to Ryan that he had just been too scared to move. He looked at his brother sternly and demanded, "Why didn't you answer when I called you?"

"I was busy looking around." Ryan was practically jumping up and down with excitement. "Isn't this a cool place? Did you see the dragonfly? I hadn't put one in. The insects, too. I never put any insects in."

"In where?" Nathan asked. "What are you talking about?" He wondered if Ryan was out of his head from shock. After all, what was happening was very unusual. It wouldn't be surprising if Ryan had snapped. Nathan felt close to snapping himself.

"I'm talking about my terrarium," Ryan said. "I put seven dinosaurs in it, that's all. But now it's full of all kinds of stuff."

Nathan looked at Ryan in wonder. He had never seen him so happy and thrilled and interested. He seemed perfectly at home.

He was still going on about his terrarium. "Maybe the insects were in the soil," he said. "And these cycads. I didn't plant any cycads. Do you think there were cycad seeds in the soil, just waiting for the right conditions for sprouting?"

Nathan batted at a cloud of humming insects that were circling above his head. "I don't know what cycads are, and I don't care," he said.

"They're these funny little palm tree things," Ryan explained.

"I said I don't care," Nathan said.

"I think that's the answer," Ryan said. "They were waiting for the right conditions, and I gave them the right conditions. I made sure the air was warm and humid, and I got real swamp soil from a real swamp—"

Nathan cut him off. "You talk like you think we're inside your terrarium."

"Well." Ryan paused. "Don't you?"

"No." Nathan said, but he didn't sound very sure.

"Then where are we?" Ryan asked. He wasn't being smart. Nathan could see that. He was just asking. But Nathan didn't have an answer.

"Well, a few minutes ago we were in my room," he said, thinking out loud.

"Our room." Ryan corrected him.

Nathan frowned at him. "Then I threw you your rock," he continued.

"Fossil egg," Ryan said.

"And you missed it, because you've never caught anything in your life," Nathan said.

"You throw wild," Ryan said.

"And the thing landed in your terrarium, and the

mist came out, and that's all I know," Nathan concluded.

"And now we're in the terrarium," Ryan said.

"We didn't get in the terrarium. It was more like—" Nathan thought a minute. "Well, it seemed like what was in the terrarium came out."

Ryan's eyes grew huge. "Do you mean my dinosaur habitat filled up our whole room? Our whole house?"

"I don't know what I mean," Nathan said.

"Our whole block?" Ryan asked. "Our whole town?"

"What we need to do," Nathan said, "is to try to find a way out."

"The whole country?" Ryan was saying. "The whole world?"

"Will you stop it?" Nathan said. "Listen to me. We've got to find a way out of here."

"What for?" Ryan threw his arms wide and spun around. "I love it here."

Then his mouth dropped open, his eyes bulged, and he started to pant. "Look," he gasped. "No. Don't move."

"I can't look if I don't move," Nathan said.

He turned to see what Ryan was staring at. Only a strong effort, and the fact that Ryan was there to see, kept him from turning tail and running. "It's a dinosaur," he said in a shaky voice. "We're dead."

8: DIPLODOCUS

"Don't talk," Ryan pleaded in a loud whisper. "Don't scare it away."

"That thing is at least twelve feet tall," Nathan said. "What could scare it?"

"It's a diplodocus," Ryan said reverently. "My diplodocus."

The dinosaur was working its way deeper into the woods, chomping on the shrubbery as it moved along. It paused, reared up on its hind legs, and stretched its neck toward a branch high overhead.

"It's gigantic," Nathan said in awe.

Ryan nodded. "I think it's the longest dinosaur there ever was."

"I know that's the ugliest shade of orange there ever was," Nathan said.

The dinosaur stripped the leaves from the branch, dropped down, and continued into the woods. It switched its whiplike tail as it moved along, knocking over ferns and cycads left and right.

Ryan started forward. "I'm going to follow it."

"Oh, no, you're not. You're going to help me find a way out of here," Nathan said. "There was a way in, so there must be a way out."

He was talking to the air. Ryan had headed straight for the huge orange shape that was disappearing into the trees. Nathan ran forward and grabbed his arm.

"Don't let it see you," he warned. "It might decide you look tastier than tree leaves."

"It's an herbivore," Ryan said. "It eats plants, not meat. Besides, it knows me. I think it will be glad to see me."

"Suppose it does know you," Nathan said. "That doesn't mean it likes you. Maybe it's had a grudge against you ever since you brought it home. Maybe it hates the terrarium. Maybe it's just been waiting for a chance like this to get back at you."

"Don't you see how big and strong and healthy it is?" Ryan asked. "It loves the terrarium. After all, I keep it warm and moist, and I put in special swamp soil—"

"If you tell me about that special swamp soil again, I'm going to push your face in it," Nathan said.

Ryan suddenly pulled away and raced over the marshy ground in the direction the dinosaur had taken.

"Come back here," Nathan shouted, but Ryan kept running, and Nathan knew he was going to have to go after him. He didn't think Ryan would get the big welcome he expected. He doubted if the dinosaur had any recollection of him, fond or otherwise. To judge by its size, it didn't have time to think about much except its next meal.

The diplodocus was out of sight, but Ryan was tracking it easily by following the path of squashed weeds. It had left footprints, too, huge, shallow bowls that rapidly filled with water.

Nathan was within an arm's length of his brother

when he sloshed through a print and left one of his sneakers in the mud on the bottom. He ran out the other side of the depression before he was able to stop himself.

"Ryan, wait, time out," he called.

Ryan ignored him. Nathan watched him go and then waded into the dinosaur footprint to find his shoe. He wasn't worried anymore about Ryan's catching the diplodocus. It was so big that even when it wasn't in a hurry, it moved along faster than a person could run. It had a good head start, too.

Nathan just hoped that Ryan didn't get lost. Not that they weren't already about as lost as you could get. And not that Ryan would care. He was having the time of his life. But Nathan had to admit to himself that he was uneasy. Nervous, actually. Well, terrified. To him there seemed to be danger everywhere you looked. But not to Ryan.

It was funny, but Nathan hadn't been as scared when Ryan showed up. He was so comfortable here. He seemed to understand the place. Things seemed more normal, or maybe just more under control, when Ryan was around.

Nathan groped around in the puddle until his fingers located his waterlogged sneaker. When he fished it out, dripping and covered with mud, he considered for a second not putting it back on. Only for a second, though. Walking around in a squishy sneaker wasn't going to be pleasant, but it was better than stepping on some big creepy bug in his socks. And there were plenty of big creepy bugs skittering around. Small creepy bugs, too.

He chose a fallen tree to sit on while he replaced his sneaker, being careful to kick at the trunk first to dislodge any insect life. Several large thousand-leggers slid out from under it and ran in all directions. Nathan shivered and sat down gingerly on the mossy log, ready to jump off if anything else came crawling along.

He shook the water out of his sneaker and was using leaves to try to wipe the mud out of it when he heard movement in the bushes some distance behind him. Good, Ryan was coming back. Not from the same direction he had run, though. He must have circled around when he saw he couldn't catch up with the diplodocus. So he hadn't gotten lost. Well, he had designed the place. Ryan was like a developer, only he had constructed an environment, instead of houses. And he called his development Dinosaur Habitat.

Nathan started to think about what a real developer would call it. While he put his shoe back on, he considered several possibilities. Big Bug Borough. Thousand-Legger Valley. Foggy Acres. Mucky Manor. He decided Mold World said it best. Actually all those names made the place sound much nicer than it really was.

As Ryan came closer, Nathan could hear him sniffing. Crying probably, because he couldn't catch up with the diplodocus. He could be such a baby sometimes.

Nathan didn't turn around. He didn't feel sorry for him. Well, maybe a little bit. But Ryan shouldn't feel sad. He should look on it as a lucky escape.

Behind Nathan the brittle leaves of the cycads rattled sharply. With each footstep the water in the dinosaur footprint quivered gently. As Nathan watched, the quiver changed to a slosh. It didn't seem as if a little kid like Ryan could shake the ground enough to do that. And those sniffing sounds. They were actually more like snuffs. Animal snuffs.

That's when Nathan knew it wasn't Ryan who had circled back. It wasn't Ryan who was behind him right now. It was the diplodocus.

9: TRICERATOPS

Nathan felt as if his body had turned to stone. He wanted to run. He wanted to yell. At the very least he wanted to turn and look. But he couldn't. Nothing was working except his brain, and the messages it was sending were too rapid and confused for his body to understand. He could only sit with his eyes wide open, staring at the water sloshing in the monster footprint.

As he stared, the sloshing gradually stopped. The rattling of the cycads ceased. Then, after another snuff or two, there was total silence.

The silence was broken by Nathan. Hot breath

behind his ear and a cool, gentle touch on his neck brought him yelping to his feet. Spinning around, he found himself face-to-face with a dinosaur. But it wasn't the diplodocus. It was much worse.

This animal wasn't as big as the other one, but it was still huge. It was all black, even its horns. Two of those horns, jutting out from above its eyes, were more than a yard long. Worst of all to Nathan, the animal had a mouth like a turtle. He felt sure it was that beak he had felt on his neck. The thought gave him the shivers.

The dinosaur snuffed softly, and Nathan began backing away as fast as he could, sliding, skidding, falling over bushes, pulling himself up and continuing backward, never taking his eyes off the animal. It watched him go, its nostrils flaring with each breath. It seemed puzzled by Nathan.

"It's probably wondering if I'm a main course or dessert," Nathan thought. He backed faster, hoping to get out of sight before the dinosaur made up its mind.

Just as the undergrowth hid the two from each other, Nathan's foot backed into thin air. He grabbed

frantically at leaves and branches, but he couldn't stop himself from falling. He landed with a sloppy thud, flat on his back in a rocky, muddy pit.

As Nathan lay there dazed, he heard a sound, an odd choking sound, coming from something in the pit with him. He knew then that he had fallen into a trap. And whatever had dug it was here, too, amazed at its luck and laughing itself silly at the sight of its prey walking backward almost into its mouth.

Nathan scrambled to his feet ready to fight or run, whichever seemed wisest. But he didn't have to choose. His pit mate wasn't a hungry dinosaur after all. It was Ryan. He was sitting in the mud, crying his head off.

It was unusual for Nathan to see his brother crying without being the cause of it himself. "What's the matter?" he asked. "Other than everything."

"They're all dead," Ryan sobbed. "And it's my fault."

Until then Nathan hadn't paid much attention to his surroundings, but now he saw what Ryan was talking about. The floor of the pit was strewn with splintered bones, pieces of leathery-looking material, and blood. Lots of blood. Nathan compared the fear he'd felt when he looked at the horned dinosaur with the fear he felt now. This fear won.

"Ryan," he said, "let's get out of here right now. "We're in a trap, and I think I just saw what dug it."

Ryan stopped crying in mid-sob. "What did you see?" he asked.

"Something big," Nathan said. "Ugly. A rhino on steroids."

Ryan's tear-covered face lit up. "With horns, right?"

"More than enough horns," Nathan said.

"That's my triceratops." Ryan jumped up. "Show it to me."

"You don't want to see it," Nathan said, "and you don't want it to see you. Look what it did to the last thing that fell in here."

"The triceratops didn't do this. It was the coelophysis." Ryan's eyes filled again. "I shouldn't have put it in. I knew they were nest robbers. But I really didn't expect to have any nests."

Nathan looked around the muddy hole they were standing in. It was about six feet across and three feet deep. "We're in a nest?" he asked.

"See the eggshells?" Ryan held up one of the leatherlike fragments. "The coelophysis ate the babies before they could hatch. It's a predator. That's what they do."

"I hope you're that understanding when it has you for a bedtime snack," Nathan said. Then he had a scary thought. "That triwhatsis wouldn't happen to be the mother of these eggs, would it?" he asked nervously.

"Right, the triceratops," Ryan said. "Its name means 'three horns.'"

"I don't care if it means 'four ears,'" Nathan said, getting more excited as he talked. "She's going to blame us for this. There are safer places for us to be right now."

But where? The triceratops was probably still nearby. And what about this coelophysis? Had the eggs satisfied its appetite or sharpened it? Nathan looked at the destruction it had left on the floor of the nest and felt very scared.

10: COELOPHYSIS

Nathan was even more scared when he saw that the mud where Ryan had been sitting was moving. A small section of the nest floor was pushing upward, dropping back, then pushing up again.

"Ryan," Nathan said.

Ryan was trying to pull himself up the slippery side of the nest. "I'm going to find my triceratops," he said.

"Just tell me this," Nathan said, watching the moving earth. "Did you put anything in your terrarium that burrows underground?"

Ryan took one look and then shoved past Nathan. He dropped to his knees and, using both hands, dug into the mud. "I think I know what this is." He was squeaking with excitement. "I hope it is. It *is!*"

He turned a radiant face to Nathan. "I'm having a baby," he said.

Nathan crouched beside Ryan to see what had made him go completely out of his head. He saw a leathery, bumpy object, maybe eight inches long, cream-colored where Ryan had scraped off the mud. The surface was covered with purple squiggles, and across the top were jagged cracks.

"The coelophysis didn't get them all," Ryan said happily. "I was sitting on it and didn't know it. I hatched it."

Nathan stood up. "Congratulations," he said. "Let's go."

Ryan's eyes were glued to the egg. "Look," he said. "Another crack. Just think, nobody's ever seen a baby dinosaur hatch before."

"If we wait to see it, we won't live to tell about it," Nathan said. "Come on."

He expected the angry mother to come plunging down into the nest at any moment, to impale them on one or more of her horns and fling them out into the swamp. It was all he could do to keep from taking off and leaving Ryan with his egg. But Ryan needed protection. No matter how smart he was, he was still a little kid.

Nathan would just have to drag him away, that was all. He was trying to decide which was the least slippery side of the nest when Ryan said, "Look!"

Nathan looked. A small hole had opened in the shell. Something twinkled in the darkness inside the egg. Then the egg rocked, and the twinkle vanished.

"That was an eye," Ryan said in a hushed voice. "A little baby dinosaur eye."

Tiny fingers reached out from within the egg and clutched the edges of broken shell. Suddenly the animal's head was free. "Oh," Ryan sighed.

Now even Nathan began to watch with interest as the little dinosaur struggled to hatch. It fought clumsily with the encircling shell. Finally, with an enormous effort, the baby heaved itself free and collapsed in the mud. It lay there motionless, except for quick, short breaths that shook its whole body.

Nathan looked at it pityingly. "It's dying," he said.

"No, it's not," Ryan said. "It's just worn out. Hatching is tiring."

"Like you would know," Nathan said.

The baby's wrinkled yellow skin seemed too big for its body. As its breathing slowed, it opened its little beaky mouth and chirped. It was so unexpected that both boys laughed.

The baby chirped again, louder, and this time there was an answering snarl from somewhere in the thick vegetation around the nest.

"That didn't sound very motherly," Nathan said, and he and Ryan nervously eyed the surrounding thicket.

Fern tops shook and cycad leaves clattered as something brushed quickly through. Suddenly a green, pointed face poked through the undergrowth, and icy eyes stared at the boys.

The face pulled back just as suddenly and then immediately appeared in another location. The animal watching them so greedily didn't seem to be very big, nothing like the diplodocus, not even as big as the triceratops, but it was scary. Its small head with the long jaws was scary, the way it stared at them with bright, cold eyes was scary, and its way of moving in sudden dashes and rushes was scary.

"Don't tell me," Nathan said. "It's the coelokiller, right?"

"See-low-fy-sis." Ryan corrected him automatically, but he looked worried. "It wants this baby."

"Are you sure it just wants the baby?" Nathan asked. "Not us?"

"Pretty sure," Ryan said. Nathan would have liked him to sound more certain.

The coelophysis, running quickly on skinny hind legs, darted out from behind the bushes. It came nearly to the nest and then sprinted back to the bushes again.

"It's a little scared of us," Ryan said.

"Not scared enough," Nathan said.

The coelophysis was starting another spring toward them when an ear-piercing shriek stopped it in its tracks. Nathan jumped a foot in the air, and Ryan grabbed the baby and held it tightly in his arms. A crashing sound coming from the swamp warned them all that something big was on its way. The coelophysis shot a last bloodthirsty look toward the nest and then sped out of sight.

"Time to go," Nathan said.

11: ESCAPE

Ryan folded the bottom of his T-shirt over the baby protectively.

"I meant the two of us," Nathan said, but a look at Ryan's face told him there was no use arguing. The baby dinosaur would be going with them. "Well, get moving," he said, and he boosted Ryan and the baby to the top of the nest. Ryan took off running, and Nathan tried to follow.

It wasn't that easy. The nest wasn't deep, but the sides were sloped and slippery. Each time Nathan took a step up, his foot slid back to the bottom again. He hadn't expected to have so much trouble, but fear and the need for haste were making him clumsy.

There were no more shrieks, but the crashing sounds continued, and Nathan made a last desperate effort to get away. He ran from one side of the nest toward the opposite bank, hoping his momentum would take him up the side before his feet began to slide again.

It almost worked. But when he was nearly at the top, a yellow, duck-faced dinosaur waddled out of the woods on its hind legs, mooing urgently.

Nathan froze. When he froze, he stopped running. When he stopped running, he slid back down into the nest. Knowing he had missed his last chance to escape, Nathan stood there, watching the approaching dinosaur.

The animal stopped mooing. It dropped onto all fours and swayed its head from side to side, as if trying for a better look.

"Maybe it has poor vision," Nathan thought hopefully. "Maybe if I stay perfectly still, it won't notice me. Maybe I'll actually live through this."

The dinosaur reared once more to its fifteen-foot height.

"Then again, maybe I won't," Nathan thought.

But he was still hopeful. The creature was looking him over, but not in the way the coelophysis had. This animal had kind eyes.

"A kind-eyed dinosaur," Nathan thought. "Now I'm thinking like Ryan."

Suddenly the dinosaur's face dipped toward him.

Nathan threw himself out of the way, but the dinosaur wasn't reaching for him. With its beaklike mouth it was exploring the remains of eggs and hatchlings that dotted the nest floor. Delicately it touched the shell that the baby had left behind.

Then the head swung toward Nathan. He tried not to flinch as the duck beak ran gently across his head, along his shoulders, and over his chest. The dinosaur mooed approvingly. Then it carefully nudged Nathan to his feet and pushed him toward the edge of the pit. It seemed obvious that it wanted him to leave the nest. What wasn't so obvious was why. Nathan wished he hadn't sent Ryan away. He had questions. Was it safe to say no to this animal, or should he cooperate? Was he dealing with an herbivore that looked on red meat with disgust? Or was this a carnivore that saw Nathan as a potential new taste treat?

Ryan would also be able to tell him if this dinosaur was an egg layer. Nathan had a feeling that this was the animal that had dug this nest. The little dinosaur that Ryan had taken away with him was probably her child. Did she know there was a live baby left? Did she think Nathan had anything to do with what had happened to her brood?

It was annoying to be so dumb about everything. Nathan felt helpless without Ryan. That was even more annoying.

The dinosaur gave up waiting for Nathan to leave the nest on his own. She wrapped her clawlike hand around him and pulled him out, then sat back on her hind legs and tail and beamed down at him. In a motherly way. As if he were her own flesh and blood. He wished she wouldn't. He wondered if she thought he was hers to keep now. There was only one way to find out.

"Well, gotta go," he said, and he tried walking casually away. It didn't work. The dinosaur dropped back to the ground, encircled his waist again, and mooed at him lovingly. Nathan could see he wasn't going anywhere.

There was rustling in the underbrush near the nest. The dinosaur released Nathan and looked toward the sound. Nathan looked, too, and saw the coelophysis staring hungrily at them through the leaves.

The duck-billed dinosaur screamed and charged.

The coelophysis leaped away into the swamp with the motherly dinosaur close behind.

As soon as she was out of sight, Nathan seized his opportunity. He flung himself in the direction Ryan had taken, running faster than he'd ever have believed he could run.

12: HADROSAUR

Nathan was moving so fast that when he heard Ryan calling his name, he continued for several yards before he could stop. He turned, chest heaving, and retraced his steps, but Ryan was nowhere in sight. Then a voice from overhead said, "Nathan," and looking up, he saw his brother high in a conifer, almost hidden in the branches.

"How did you get up there?" he asked.

"I don't know," Ryan said. "I was just so scared."

Nathan almost laughed. It was amazing what fear could do. He was sure he had just broken all sprinting records, and unathletic Ryan had managed to climb up a swaying, prickly, buggy tree while carrying a squirming newly hatched dinosaur.

"Where have you been?" Ryan asked. "I thought you were right behind me."

"I've been adopted," Nathan said. "Come on down. I want to get more distance between us and that nest."

Ryan had a lot more trouble coming down than he had probably had going up. "Ouch. Ouch," he kept saying as the evergreen needles stuck into him. When he was close enough, he handed the baby dinosaur to Nathan and let himself drop to the ground.

"What do you mean, you're adopted?" he asked.

Nathan was examining the baby. It was larger than he had thought. Stretched out, it was more than a foot long. And although its beak was shorter and its color was paler, it was obvious that the affectionate animal Nathan had just been with was its mother.

The baby twisted and squirmed in his hands, squeaking loudly.

"How do you hold on to this thing?" Nathan asked.

Ryan held out his arms. The baby leaped to him and settled down contentedly. Ryan chuckled. "It thinks I'm its mother," he said.

"I'm not surprised," Nathan said. "Its real mother thinks I'm her baby."

"You saw the triceratops again," Ryan said, looking disappointed, "and I've never seen it once."

Nathan shook his head. "Not that one. I'm talking about the dinosaur with a face like a duck."

"A duckbill?" Ryan asked excitedly. "Then this is a baby hadrosaur." He looked closely at the little animal he was holding. "I should have known that's what it was. But when you saw that triceratops, it threw me off. They both lay eggs, you know."

"How would I know a thing like that?" Nathan asked. "What I do know is that if she hadn't gone after the coelokiller, I'd be leading the life of a baby hardeehar right now."

"Hadrosaur." Ryan corrected him. "Coelophysis."

A loud wail from out of the swamp made them all jump.

"Wow," Ryan said. "I wonder which one that was."

The wail was repeated, a terrible, sad sound that

sent chills down Nathan's back. He had no doubt at all which one it was.

"It's the duckbill," he said. "She's looking for me."

"It might not be the duckbill," Ryan said. "There are other dinosaurs here, remember?"

"No, it's the duck," Nathan said. "She loves me. She'll look until she finds me."

The wailing cry floated over the treetops, and the baby hadrosaur braced its front feet against Ryan's shoulder and looked around with interest. Ryan put the little animal on the ground. It stood facing away from them, sending chirping notes into the swamp.

"See," Nathan said. "It knows a hardeehar when it hears one."

"Hadrosaur," Ryan said glumly. "I guess we should take it back."

"How can we take it back?" Nathan asked. "I can't go near that nest. She'll get me."

"I'll do it," Ryan said.

"I don't know whether you should try it," Nathan said. "Not that I think she's dangerous. In fact, I believe she'd make a very nice mother. But we already have one. Somewhere."

"It'll be okay. She'll know her baby when she sees it," Ryan said. "They should be together."

He looked so sad that Nathan felt sorry for him. He tried to think of something to say to cheer him up. "You'll be making a dinosaur very happy," he told Ryan. "How often does that opportunity come along?"

Ryan's face brightened a little. "Hardly ever," he said.

He picked up the little dinosaur and turned away. Nathan watched him squish into the swamp, the baby happily nibbling the neck of his T-shirt as they moved along.

13: PTEROSAUR

As soon as Ryan was out of sight, Nathan began to wish he had gone along. What if they lost each other again? It would be easy to do in a place that was nothing but various-size plants in various shades of green. The swamp was like a huge salad bar, but one where the salad does the eating.

The insects were doing their share of eating, too. Nathan itched all over. He was busy trying to scratch everywhere at once when Ryan came into sight, running fast, without the baby. He grabbed Nathan and dragged him toward a low, thick bush.

"Get under here quick," he panted. "We've got to hide."

Nathan didn't stop to ask why. With Ryan, he forced his way under the stiff, leafy branches. Several needle-nosed bugs joined them, but Nathan hardly noticed. "Is the mother after you?" he whispered. "Is she mad because you took her baby?"

"She wasn't there," Ryan whispered back. "I left the baby by the nest."

"Then why are we hiding?" Nathan asked.

"Shh," Ryan said. "I'm afraid it might try to follow me."

Just then a little dinosaur nose pushed through the leaves. "It found me," Ryan said. "Looks like we'll have to keep it." Nathan could see that he was trying not to appear too happy about it.

They crawled out of their hiding place, and the baby pranced away, looking back at Ryan as if inviting him to play.

"Let it go," Nathan said. "Maybe it'll get lost."

"It's headed for the lake," Ryan said. "Come on. We haven't seen my lake yet." He ran after the baby.

After a moment Nathan followed, just because he didn't know what else to do. Ryan was already out of sight, but through breaks in the foliage Nathan could see a glitter that must be the lake. By the time he reached the shore, Ryan had undressed and was heading for the water.

"Should you be running around here naked?" Nathan asked.

"Yes!" Ryan shouted, and he splashed into the lake. He swam a little and then floated on his back, letting the water wash away the mud that covered his arms and legs. "Come on, Nathan," he called. "It feels good."

The baby dinosaur didn't like so much space between it and Ryan. It stood belly deep in the water, calling to him with junior versions of the wails the mother had made when she was looking for Nathan. Nathan wished it wouldn't. The sounds might attract trouble. There was an ornery-looking coelophysis out there, which was bad enough, but there was also a hadrosaur that knew she was a mother but wasn't clear on the child.

Nathan pulled off his shoes and socks and went after the baby. He picked it up, saying, "Stop your screeching," but it wriggled free and launched itself into the water. When Ryan saw it coming, he swam to meet it, and the two of them waded back to shore.

"Isn't this perfect?" Ryan said. "It's just the way I planned it."

"Should that mountain be smoking like that?" Nathan asked.

"Sure. It's a volcano," Ryan said. "I told you I made a volcano."

While he admired his handiwork and the baby splashed nearby, Nathan was looking at the cliff across from the volcano. Something sitting on a ledge had begun to move. As Nathan watched, it stretched out a long neck and raised tremendous wings.

"Ryan, look, a birdosaur," he said as the creature,

looking as big as an airplane, leaped into space and soared in a slow circle above the lake.

"That's my pterosaur," Ryan said. He didn't sound as happy as Nathan would have expected. In fact, he sounded a little worried.

The pterosaur had stopped circling and was gliding swiftly in their direction. "Should we be running?" Nathan asked. Then he saw what Ryan had already realized. The animal wasn't concerned with them at all. Its long, thin head on its long, thin neck was aimed straight for the baby dinosaur.

"No!" Ryan shouted. He ran and threw himself on top of the little hadrosaur. And Nathan, yelling at the top of his lungs, threw himself on top of Ryan.

The giant bird attacked. But instead of the mouthful of baby hadrosaur it had intended to carry off, it swooped back into the air with Nathan's T-shirt hanging from its bill—and Nathan entangled in the shirt.

14: PLESIOSAUR

The weight of Nathan dangling from its beak affected the bird's ability to gain altitude, so when the shirt ripped, dumping Nathan into the water, he didn't have far to fall. He sputtered to the surface, glad that he could swim, because he was far out on the lake. He scanned the sky and saw the bird, the T-shirt still tangled in its beak, heading back to its perch.

Ryan was watching from the shore, holding the little hadrosaur in his arms. Nathan waved to show that he was all right. He could tell that Ryan was torn between wanting to see more of the giant bird and wanting to keep the baby safe from it. Concern for the baby won out. Ryan crawled under the trunk of a fallen palm, pulling the little animal with him.

Nathan treaded water while he watched the bird land on its ledge. It shook its head and rubbed its beak against the cliff wall, trying to dislodge the T-shirt. Nathan decided to head for shore before it was ready for another hunting trip.

He hadn't gone more than a few strokes when he had the feeling that he wasn't swimming alone. He tried to tell himself that it was his imagination, that the movement he saw from the corner of his eye was just his own splashing. But he knew that something was there. He could sense it gliding beside him, just below the surface of the water. He seemed to see its shadow, sometimes on his left, sometimes on his right, but always close by.

"It's probably just waterweeds," he told himself, but he wasn't convinced. He tried to swim faster, but his wet jeans were heavy, and they slowed him down. He knew he would do better without them, but he wasn't sure he could swim and undress at the same time.

Before he could find out, his foot kicked against something under the water, something solid and slippery. Something alive. Nathan gave up the idea of getting rid of his jeans. All he had on his mind now was reaching shore in one piece. "Don't think; just swim," he told himself firmly.

Then, only a few yards away, the shadow showed itself. A head, all big, wet eyes and spiky teeth, broke the surface of the water. Held up by a long, snaky neck, it rose dripping into the air.

Nathan tried not to look. He felt very close to panic, and he knew that if he panicked, he would sink like a stone. He continued to swim steadily toward shore, all the while uncomfortably aware of that head swaying above him. Then, abruptly, the creature sank and disappeared.

Before Nathan had time to hope it had gone away, it popped back up, and this time it leaped completely out of the water. Nathan had only a quick look at the whole animal before it smashed back down into the lake. But that brief glimpse was enough to see that the long neck was attached to a body shaped like a huge keg with flippers.

Nathan began to swim with all his might, until all at once his arms were flailing through air, not water. For a crazy second he thought he must be flying. Then he realized that the animal had come up underneath him, and he was sprawled on top of its broad blue back. Gracefully it looped its neck to bring its face close to Nathan's, giving him a close look at its big, mischievous eyes and its way-too-many teeth.

At the approach of those teeth Nathan threw himself back into the water. The creature was under him immediately, lifting him out again. Nathan saw that there was no way to escape. All he could do was try to look as unappetizing as possible. This time, when the animal turned to look at him, Nathan stared back as fiercely as he could. He felt like a kitten trying to scare a pit bull.

The animal began to sink. It submerged gradually until Nathan was floating free. He started to tread water, but the animal rose under him again, so that once more Nathan was lying on its back. Again it brought its face, with those terrible teeth and laughing eyes, close to Nathan's face. Suddenly Nathan realized what was happening.

"This thing is playing," he thought in amazement. "It's not trying to hurt me. It's having fun."

15: WATER GAMES

Over and over the animal dropped away from Nathan and then lifted him again. He found that he didn't even have to tread water or make any effort to stay afloat. The creature always caught him before he could sink.

Nathan didn't notice when it happened, but his fear dissolved, and he began to enjoy himself. The water rinsed off the swamp mud and soothed his itches. It was fun to slide into the warm lake, knowing that his living raft would be there to lift him up again.

The only problem was that mosses or some kinds of little organisms were growing in patches on the animal's back. Ryan would be interested, no doubt. He would probably say they were things he hadn't put in the terrarium. But they made the creature's skin very slippery. Nathan inched himself up the animal's body until he reached a place on its neck that was narrow enough for him to wrap his arms around. Now he felt more secure. The creature looked back at him, grinned a toothy grin, and dived.

Nathan wasn't prepared. He was almost torn from the animal's neck by the surging water. But as the creature glided to the surface, Nathan's feet found the place where its thick front flippers came out of its body. He braced himself, one leg on either side, and hung on.

It was the ride of a lifetime. The creature dived, leaped, crashed down again, sped like a speedboat along the surface of the lake. As he clung to its neck, his feet braced against its front flippers, Nathan seemed to be a part of the animal. He almost felt like the animal itself. He shouted with excitement as he soared upward. Underwater he clung tightly as they rolled and spun dizzily. He never had to gasp for breath. He didn't know whether it was for his benefit or if the animal itself needed oxygen, but they always surfaced well before he felt the need for air.

Nathan thought he could go on like this forever. Skimming across the water, plunging into its depths, exploding into the sky—he had never known anything could be so exciting. He forgot he had ever been afraid of this place. He forgot about wanting to go home. In fact, he felt that he *was* home, that this was where he belonged.

A loud boom broke the spell. Instantly the animal stopped its game and floated on the surface of the lake, rocking in water that had suddenly become rough.

There was another boom, and now Nathan realized that the noise was coming from the volcano. The animal stretched its neck, raising its head high in the air as it gazed at the huge black cloud forming over the mountain. Nathan could feel its body quiver. It paddled toward the volcano, then away, then in large circles, seeming disoriented and undecided. It looped its neck and peered sadly into Nathan's face.

"Oh, no," Nathan thought. "It's saying good-bye."

The creature turned toward shore and swam as close as it could without becoming grounded. Then it slipped out from under Nathan and disappeared.

Nathan treaded water for a minute, hoping it would come back. But it didn't. The ride was over. Feeling as if he had lost a friend, Nathan swam back to shore.

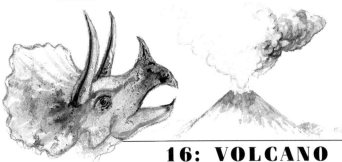

16: VOLCANO

When Nathan reached land, he ran toward the downed tree where Ryan had taken refuge. He found him examining some tiny plants growing in the muck, while the baby slept peacefully beside him.

"Ryan, you missed it," he said.

"Is it back?" Ryan asked fearfully. The baby woke up and squeaked, and he gave it a warning shush.

"What, the birdosaur?" Nathan said. "No, it's sitting on its ledge tearing up my T-shirt."

"It's not a bird," Ryan said. "It's not a dinosaur, either. It's a pterosaur."

"What's it doing here if it's not a dinosaur?" For

a minute Nathan forgot that Ryan had made this place and stocked it himself.

"It came with the set," Ryan told him.

"Oh. Well, so far I like the fishosaur best," Nathan said.

"There's no such thing as a fishosaur," Ryan said.

"Then what was I playing with out there?" Nathan asked.

Ryan jumped up and rushed out to the shore. He looked eagerly out across the water. "Where is it?" he demanded. "Where's my plesiosaur?"

"If you mean a big blue friendly animal with flippers, I don't exactly know," Nathan said, "but it's under there somewhere."

Ryan frowned. "This is *my* world," he said, "and *you're* seeing all the animals."

"Not because I want to," Nathan said. "Although I'm glad I ran into the fishosaur. We had a good time."

"It's called a plesiosaur," Ryan said. "It's not a fish, and it's not a dinosaur."

"It seems to me you put a lot of non-dinosaurs in your dinosaur habitat," Nathan said.

"I told you, it was a set," Ryan said. "It had a variety of animals in it to make it more interesting."

"I guess that's why they painted them all those crazy colors, too," Nathan said. "To get people's attention."

"I'm the one who painted them." Ryan sounded a little huffy. "I think they're pretty. Nobody knows what colors they really were, anyway, so what's the difference?"

"Hmm," Nathan said. "You're not as scientific as I thought."

"I just made the kind of place I'd like to live in," Ryan told him.

"Well, it's not the kind of place *I'd* like to live in," Nathan said. Then he remembered the way he'd felt when he was swimming with the plesiosaur. He hadn't wanted that to ever end. But it had.

"We have to go home," he said.

Ryan was staring at the water as if he could make the plesiosaur appear if he looked hard enough. "I don't want to go home," he said without turning around. "Besides, we don't know how."

"We have to try," Nathan said.

"No, we don't," Ryan said obstinately.

A loud explosion came from the volcano, and the size of the black cloud over the mountain doubled.

"Yes, we do," Nathan said.

17: DISCOVERY

"It isn't going to erupt, if that's what you're thinking," Ryan said.

"It's a volcano, isn't that what you told me?" Nathan asked.

"It's just to look at, though," Ryan said. "Not to blow up."

"You may be the designer and builder of Mold World, but you're not the one running it," Nathan said. "What about the bugs? You said you didn't put them in. But they're here. What about this baby? You didn't put *it* in. If your hardeehar can lay eggs, your volcano can erupt."

"Hadrosaur," Ryan said. "Okay I'll help look for a way out. But that doesn't mean I'll go if we find one."

Nathan suspected that Ryan only wanted to have a way to get the baby out of danger in an emergency, but at least he was going to cooperate. His reasons didn't matter.

"Do you have any ideas?" he asked. It seemed backward for him to be asking little Ryan for advice. Nathan felt as if he were visiting a foreign country where Ryan had lived all his life.

"Nope," Ryan said cheerfully.

Neither did Nathan. He didn't know how he'd gotten in, so how could he find his way out? "Well, let's start by looking around," he said. "We really haven't done much exploring."

"Okay," Ryan said. He dressed while Nathan pulled on his soggy socks and sneakers.

They left the lakeside and plunged back into the swamp. "It seems quiet," Nathan said. "I wonder what happened to the duckbill."

"I don't know," Ryan said. "Maybe she has a short memory. Maybe she's forgotten about her baby."

"I just hope she's forgotten about *me*," Nathan said.

They were walking too slowly for the baby hadro-

saur. It scampered back and forth on little side trips of its own, until an object protruding from the mud caught its attention. It circled the thing cautiously, examining it with great interest.

"I wonder what it has," Ryan said. He ran ahead to look, but after one glance he scooped up the baby and hurried back to Nathan. "That's not a good way to go," he said. He started walking quickly in the opposite direction.

"Wait," Nathan said. "What was it? What did you see?"

"Nothing. Come on." Ryan was so flustered that Nathan became suspicious. He hadn't been particularly interested in whatever was lying up ahead, but he was now. He jogged over to look, and there, half buried in mud, was the discovery that Ryan was trying to keep to himself.

The baby had found the terrarium.

18: ERUPTION

Ryan's terrarium was empty of animals and plants, but it was still in one piece, and the fossil was still inside. Nathan could see remnants of gray mist floating across its surface.

Now he knew that they weren't inside the terrarium. Until this minute he hadn't been completely sure. But he was puzzled. Why was Ryan so anxious to keep him away from it? What was here that he didn't want Nathan to see?

Ryan appeared beside him. "See, it's nothing," he said.

"Why did you try to hide it?" Nathan asked.

"I didn't try to hide it," Ryan protested, looking completely guilty. "Come on, let's explore some more."

Nathan looked hard into his face. Why was he acting this way? What was worrying him? "I think I'll just explore the terrarium first," he said.

"No, come on, Nathan." Ryan was insistent. "It's probably not a real fossil, anyway, just an old rock."

At that moment Nathan knew what was the matter with Ryan. His words had given him away. Nathan looked from his brother to the fossil and back again. "You believe that rock caused all this, don't you?" he said. "You've thought it all along."

Ryan saw that he had made a mistake. "No, I haven't," he said confusedly. "Did I say that? I didn't say that."

"You're no good at lying, Ryan," Nathan told him.

"Yes, I am," Ryan said.

Nathan laughed. It was good to have his clueless little brother back. Ryan as all-knowing biologist had been hard to take sometimes.

"So you think that your fossil brought us to prehistory and that it can send us back," Nathan said.

"No, I think it's just a rock," Ryan said stubbornly.

"Oh, okay," Nathan said. "Then it won't matter if I just take it out of the terrarium and throw it away, will it?"

Ryan became very agitated. "No, don't touch it," he pleaded.

"Why not?" Nathan asked. "Tell me the truth about that fossil, Ryan, or I'm going to dump the terrarium."

Nathan wasn't being quite truthful himself. He really didn't want to dump the terrarium. He was nervous about what might happen. It might be nothing. That would be bad enough. Or they might end up in an even worse state than they were now. He didn't want to be responsible for that. He stood there watching the fossil send out its mysterious vapor while he waited for Ryan to answer.

"I don't know for sure," Ryan said finally, "but I'm afraid it will change everything. I'm afraid that if you take my fossil out of the terrarium, we'll end up back home."

"That's the whole idea, Ryan," Nathan told him. "We've got to get back home."

"I never want to go home." Ryan's gaze went from the spongy earth to the thick, dripping foliage to the tall, mossy trees. "I want to stay here forever."

Nathan knew that Ryan really believed what he was saying. He was starting to understand how much this place meant to his little brother. A world he had dreamed about all his life had become real, and he was part of it. Nathan could see why he didn't want to leave. But Nathan did. And since he couldn't leave without Ryan, Ryan was going, too—as soon as Nathan figured out how.

There was a booming sound, and the air seemed to shake around them. A fiery red substance surged over the rim of the volcanic cone and spilled down the side of the mountain. From where they stood, it looked like a river of blood, but Nathan knew that it was really molten rock. He watched fearfully as it streamed down the mountainside.

"You were right!" Ryan shouted joyfully. "My volcano is really erupting!"

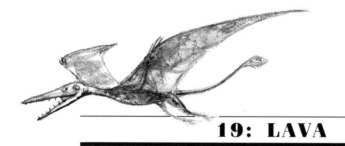

19: LAVA

"What are you so happy about?" Nathan said. "That red stuff isn't strawberry jelly, you know."

Ryan nodded. "I know. It's lava."

"That's right, lava," Nathan said. "Lava is hot. It can move fast. Let's go."

He reached for the fossil and then found himself afraid to touch it. If it really had the powers he suspected, it was dangerous. What if it was red-hot? What if it exploded? He reminded himself that he had held it in his hand not long ago without incident. But that was before everything else happened.

The volcano thundered again, and the earth trembled. Nathan decided that whatever the fossil did to him couldn't be any worse than a lava bath.

His fingers touched the rock, and instantly he felt himself thrown off his feet. He hit the ground hard and stayed there for a few seconds, dazed. His first thought was that touching the fossil had somehow caused him to fall. Then he saw Ryan watching him with a scared but determined expression on his face, and he realized that his little brother had knocked him down.

Ryan looked as surprised as Nathan. He backed away as Nathan got to his feet, but Nathan wasn't going to waste time trading punches.

"Give it up, Ryan," he said. "We can't hang around here any longer. It's too dangerous."

"It's not dangerous," Ryan argued. "Not yet. Look, the lava is sliding down into the lake."

Nathan looked toward the volcano. The crimson river was wider now, and other smaller rivers had branched off and were flowing down on either side of it. All the streams were pouring into the lake, causing huge clouds of steam to rise and spread over the water.

"That doesn't make me feel any better," he said. "What happens when the lake is full?" He held out one hand to fend off Ryan and reached into the terrarium with the other.

"Wait! Let me get the baby." Ryan caught the little dinosaur up in his arms and stood braced for whatever might happen next.

"What are you doing?" Nathan said. "You can't take that animal home."

"I have to," Ryan said determinedly. "It needs me. I'm almost its mother."

"Ryan, let me tell you something," Nathan said. "That is a prehistoric animal. You are a historic boy.

You belong back home. The baby belongs here."

Ryan burst out crying. "It's too little to be left alone. The coelophysis will get it."

Instead of feeling mad at Ryan, the way he usually did when he cried, Nathan felt sorry. It *was* sad to have to leave the little dinosaur by itself. But what could they do? They couldn't stick around until the baby was able to take care of itself. That might be months. Years even.

Then Nathan thought of the obvious solution. It wasn't without its risks. But then, they'd faced one risk after another ever since they had landed in this place. What was one more?

20: CHIRPS

Nathan glanced at the lava, which was still flowing into the water. So far the lake was able to contain it. "Ryan," he said firmly, "stop crying. We're not going to leave until the baby is safe with its mother, okay?"

"We tried that." Ryan gulped. "It didn't work."

"That's because we didn't do it right," Nathan said. "We can't just dump the baby and run. We have to bring the two of them together. Once they see each other, they'll forget all about you and me."

Ryan looked a little sulky. He didn't really want the little hadrosaur to forget him. "We don't know where the mother is," he said.

"No problem," Nathan said. "We'll just make the baby cry. Its mother will hear and come running."

"No!" Ryan clasped the baby so tightly that it squeaked.

"Like that," Nathan said.

"I'm not going to let you hurt this baby," Ryan said.

"Just a few pinches?" Nathan asked.

"No." Ryan was very definite.

"How about if I tickle it then?" Nathan said. "It's for its own good, you know."

Ryan reluctantly put the little animal on the ground. "No rough stuff," he warned.

Nathan tried his best. He tickled the baby under its arms and under its chin. He rolled it over and tickled its belly. He even tickled the soles of its feet.

The baby loved it. Again and again it wiggled away and shook itself and then came running back for more. But aside from a few snorts and a couple of moos, it didn't make a sound.

Nathan played out before the little hadrosaur did. "This isn't working," he said. "We'll have to try something else."

"No pinching," Ryan said.

"No, I have a better idea," Nathan said. "I'll imitate its voice."

Ryan looked at him skeptically. "You can't sound like a hadrosaur."

"It doesn't have to be good," Nathan said. "I don't *look* like one, either, but she thought I was her baby." He attempted a few squeaks.

Ryan burst out laughing. "That's terrible!"

"Well, let's hear you do it better," Nathan said.

"Well, sometimes it chirps like this." Ryan tried to duplicate the sound.

Now it was Nathan's turn to laugh. "That's not a

chirp. This is a chirp," he said, giving his own version.

Ryan hooted. "Your chirp is worse than my chirp," he said, making another attempt.

Nathan snorted. "Your chirp is more of a squeal," he said.

Over and over they tried to imitate the little dinosaur's calls, and the more they chirped, the more they laughed. The baby looked from one to the other, fascinated. Suddenly it added its own chirps to theirs. Ryan threw himself to the ground, giggling and chirping at the same time, and the baby climbed onto his chest, calling excitedly into his face.

Nathan was laughing so hard that he had almost forgotten the purpose of making the silly sounds. He was still chirping away when the baby slid off Ryan's chest and stared intently into the trees. Ryan sat up and looked in the same direction. "You can stop chirping now," he said.

"I'm just getting the hang of it," Nathan said.

Then he heard what the others were listening to. Anxious mooing calls were coming closer with every crashing footstep. The mother hadrosaur had gotten the message.

21: STAMPEDE

As its mother came closer, the baby began to run back and forth, uttering a series of loud squeaks.

"She'll think we're killing it," Nathan said nervously.

But the hadrosaur burst into view with eyes only for her baby. The little dinosaur flung itself at her, chirping ecstatically. The mother examined it carefully with her duck beak, nuzzling and nibbling while the baby squeaked and rolled at her feet. Finally she flopped to the ground and lay there contentedly as the baby played on her massive body, clambering over her back, sliding down her tail, and burrowing under her neck. Nathan and Ryan stood by, feeling a little left out.

"She should be embarrassed to look at me after the dumb mistake she made," Nathan said. "How could she think I was a baby hardeehar?"

He waited for Ryan to correct his pronunciation,

but there was silence. He glanced at his brother and saw that he was gulping hard, trying not to cry. Nathan went over and threw an arm across his shoulders. "Don't feel bad, Ryan," he said. "It all worked out for the best."

Ryan leaned against Nathan and rubbed at his eyes with his fists. "I liked that little baby," he said in a choked voice. "We had fun together."

Nathan pulled his brother's hands away from his face and held him by the shoulders. "Look," he said, "now we can go home with clear consciences. We're not deserting the baby. It's perfectly happy and safe."

"But I wanted to take it with me," Ryan said.

"It would be nothing but trouble," Nathan told him. "It's going to grow. You see the size of its mother."

"Maybe they grow slow," Ryan said.

"Maybe," Nathan said, "but eventually you wouldn't be able to keep it in the house."

"I could tie it up outside," Ryan said.

"You'd need a truck to cart away what it would do in the grass every day," Nathan said. He was glad to hear Ryan giggle. "And if it got loose, which it would," he went on, "it would eat every tree, bush, flower bed, and vegetable garden in the neighborhood."

"And when it got mad, it would scream the way its mother did at the coelophysis," Ryan said, getting caught up in Nathan's predictions. "Everybody would be scared to death."

They both were chuckling, enjoying the thought of the neighborhood's reaction to the hadrosaur's lifestyle, when they heard something smashing through the swamp. They stopped laughing and stared as the triceratops broke into view and thundered past, so close that they could hear its snorting breath. Within seconds the diplodocus followed, pounding its way through the woods.

"They're running from the lava," Nathan said.

"No," Ryan said in a voice that shook with excitement. "They're not running from the lava. They're running from *that*."

Nathan looked where he was pointing and gasped. Coming toward them, following the path the fleeing animals had taken, was a gigantic, glittering carnivore.

22: TYRANNOSAURUS

Nathan knew the animal was a carnivore because its enormous jaws hung open, showing a mouthful of what looked like an assortment of knives. They were definitely not grass-chewing teeth.

"My tyrannosaurus," Ryan said in delight.

"I think we'd have a better chance against the lava," Nathan said, starting to back away.

The tyrannosaurus had tiny front legs, but that was the only tiny thing about it. Its oversize head was longer than Ryan was tall, and its thighs made tree trunks look like skinny sticks. As the creature strolled along on its hind legs, its skin shimmered brilliantly.

"That color is called metallic gold," Ryan said. "Isn't it perfect?"

Nathan didn't bother to answer. How could Ryan stand there bragging about his paint job at a time like this?

The tyrannosaurus was taking its time, as if it enjoyed the panic it was causing. The hadrosaurs had been watching with curiosity as the other dinosaurs raced through the swamp. Now the mother caught sight of the approaching carnivore. She lurched to her feet and, mooing loudly, urged the baby toward the boys. Before Nathan understood what she was planning, he found himself and Ryan being half pushed and half carried into the swamp, while the baby danced along beside them.

"She's trying to save us," Ryan said. "Isn't she brave?"

Nathan couldn't respond. He was too busy trying to extricate himself from the animal's loving claws. It was nice that she cared, but Nathan wanted to escape from more than the metallic gold monster. His real goal was to get out of this dinosaur habitat completely. But he needed the fossil for that, and now, with every step, he was being dragged farther and farther from it.

Then, in a green blur, the nest-robbing coelophysis streaked by, snarling to itself as it ran. It didn't even glance their way, but to the mother hadrosaur it signaled danger. She reared up and screamed threaten-ingly after it.

Suddenly Nathan was free. He turned and ran straight for the place where the terrarium was lying, even though it also meant running straight toward the tyrannosaurus. But when he reached the spot, he found nothing but a clump of reeds. The terrarium was gone.

23: TALONS

It couldn't be gone. Nathan ran frantically in circles, searching the ground. He must have gotten turned around somehow. With nothing but trees and cycads and ferns for landmarks, everything looked alike. He suspected that he was searching the same places over and over, but he didn't know what else to do.

The tyrannosaurus was close now, much too close. The mother hadrosaur was watching its approach, emitting shriek after shriek, while Ryan and the baby peered from behind her legs. In a brief glance their way, Nathan saw that Ryan actually looked worried. That scared him more than anything that had happened yet. Desperately he resumed his search. At last, by pure dumb luck, he stumbled on the terrarium.

At the same moment a giant chicken foot equipped with sharp, terrible claws slammed down in front of him. Nathan didn't look up. He didn't have to. He knew that the tyrannosaurus was there, towering above him.

"Run, Nathan!" Ryan screamed.

More than anything else, running was what Nathan wanted to do. But first there was the fossil. He snatched it up and with all his strength threw it out into the swamp.

Instantly the shreds of mist that still drifted like ghosts through the trees began to move in the direction of the soaring rock. Nathan had a glimpse of Ryan running toward it. He saw him leap like an outfielder, arms outstretched, and then the mist, swirling up from the ground, writhing away from the treetops, enclosed everything in a gray-white cloud.

Nathan heard the tyrannosaurus bellow. Out of the haze above him a taloned foot appeared. Nathan stared straight up at it, and as the foot came toward him, he fell over on his back, arms over his face.

There was time to realize that in an instant he was going to be crushed by a huge golden dinosaur. But there was no time to get away.

24: HOME

Nathan braced himself for the impact. He hoped he wouldn't be too squashed. Maybe the ground was soft enough to let him sink into it when the weight of the tyrannosaurus pressed down on him. He pulled his arms tighter across his face and squeezed his eyes shut. But the foot didn't come down.

He lay still, wondering. Had the animal gone? Was he really going to get out of being stepped on? Or had it already happened? Maybe he was dead. He didn't feel dead, not that he was any judge. He did feel different, though. Cooler. Drier. And nothing was biting him.

He moved his arms slightly, just enough to peek through. There was no animal above him. There were no trees, no floating mist. Nothing but his bedroom ceiling.

Slowly he sat up and looked around. He really was home, really back in his own bedroom. His and Ryan's. Nothing had changed. Ryan's junk was still everywhere. The terrarium was still against the wall under the window. Ryan was there, kneeling beside it.

Nathan shook his head, trying to clear it of a sense of unreality. He got up, feeling a little shaky, and went to stand beside Ryan. "Did that really happen?" he thought.

Here in their bedroom, where everything was so ordinary and normal, it seemed impossible. But when he looked in the terrarium, where Ryan was removing little broken branches and straightening tilted trees, he knew that it really had. It gave him a strange feeling to look down into the world that had been so vast and frightening. It was small and quiet now, but it was the same world.

There was the mountain, asleep again. There was the rocky cliff where the pterosaur perched.

The triceratops stood by the glassy lake. Nathan remembered the inquisitive touch of that turtle beak on the back of his neck. He wondered what would have happened if he hadn't been so afraid. What if he had stayed and tried to make friends with the animal?

He knew there was no question of making friends with the coelophysis. It didn't have the temperament. Nathan looked until he found it skulking in the under-brush, its green color blending with the surrounding foliage.

The bright orange diplodocus was easy to spot, and so was the yellow hadrosaur, as she stood guard over her nest, a nest that was no longer empty. Nathan glanced at Ryan, hoping he wasn't too sad about leaving the baby, but Ryan didn't seem sad at all.

Nathan was the one who was feeling sad. He reached down and picked up the barrel-shaped plesio-saur. He held it in his palm, remembering the trusting friendliness of the real animal and the thrill of their game in the warm blue lake.

"It's crazy," he told Ryan. "The whole time we were slogging around in your swamp, all I could think about was getting out. Now I almost wish I could go back."

Ryan didn't comment. He was being very busy with the terrarium. For someone who had been ready to fight to stay in his prehistoric paradise, he seemed surprisingly reconciled to being back home. Nathan watched him thoughtfully. How could he be so calm about leaving a place he loved so much? Nathan could think of only one reason. Ryan must know that he could get back there again.

25: WAITING

Nathan knelt beside Ryan and tried to catch his eye. "So," he said conversationally, "it really was the fossil that moved us around."

Ryan didn't look up. "Looks like it," he murmured.

"Too bad we don't have it anymore," Nathan said.

"Yeah," Ryan said. He moved his shoulders uncomfortably.

"When I threw it, I saw you jump for it," Nathan said, "but then it got foggy. I didn't see if you caught it."

Ryan looked at him warily. "I can't catch, you know that."

"I know you can't," Nathan said. "But you know what, Ryan? I think this time you did."

"No, Nathan" was all Ryan had time to say before his brother jumped him. Ryan screamed as Nathan held him down and went through his pockets. When Nathan pulled out the fossil, Ryan screamed louder and began kicking and punching so wildly that Nathan was afraid to let him up. "Calm down," he gasped. "Here, take your rock back. You're more dangerous than the tyrannosaurus."

Ryan grabbed the rock, and they both sat up, breathing hard. Ryan glared fiercely at Nathan and held himself ready for another tussle, but when Nathan didn't make any more moves toward the fossil, he began to relax. "You can't stop me from going back," he said.

"I'm not going to stop you," Nathan said, "but you can't go alone. I have to be there to keep an eye on you."

He felt a little silly saying that. He hadn't exactly been the Hero of Dinosaur Habitat. But he would be braver this time. He knew what to expect now: hungry dinosaurs and an active volcano. On second thought he wasn't sure how much braver he was going to be. But scared or not, he had to go along to make sure that Ryan came home again.

"I didn't think you'd want to go back," Ryan said. "I didn't think you liked it."

"Neither did I," Nathan admitted. "I'm still not sure."

Ryan hopped to his feet. "Let's go now," he said.

"Not so soon," Nathan said, laughing. "I'm still not over the first trip yet."

"Well, when?" Ryan demanded. "Tonight? To-morrow?"

Nathan shook his head. "I have to do some research first. I don't want to have to depend on you for every-thing next time."

"I can't wait," Ryan complained. He collected books from his bed and the floor and the bookcase and threw them into Nathan's lap. "Read fast," he said.

Nathan flipped through some pages. In a way it was like looking at his own vacation album. He stopped at a picture of a plesiosaur and read the description.

"They don't mention how friendly it is," he said.

"You're the only one who knows that," Ryan said. "I didn't even get to see it."

"When we go back, you can swim with it," Nathan said. He felt a rush of excitement, and suddenly he was as impatient as his brother to see their prehistoric world again. He settled down to some serious reading.

Ryan roamed restlessly, tossing the fossil from hand to hand. Finally, he sat beside the terrarium and adjusted the lid carefully, as he always did, so that the inhabitants would have just the right amount of air and light and humidity. Then he sat quietly, waiting for Nathan to be ready to go.

Inside the terrarium, silent and still, the wet green world was waiting, too.